T0368431

Written By Marissa Rose Aulick

DEDICATION

This book is lovingly dedicated to:

My Grandma Rose, who first taught me the importance of respecting the wisdom of my elders—albeit, learned the hard way. (A story for another day.) ☺

My Aunt Ertha, whose example of sacrificial love for family, hard work, and strength continues to motivate me today.

And to my children's paternal grandparents, Randy and Lou, whose intentional and active role in helping Andrew and me "raise our children to rise" is a blessing beyond measure.

WestBow Press books may be ordered through booksellers or by contacting:

WestBow Press
A Division of Thomas Nelson & Zondervan
1663 Liberty Drive
Bloomington, IN 47403
www.westbowpress.com
844-714-3454

Because of the dynamic nature of the Internet, any web addresses or links contained in this book may have changed since publication and may no longer be valid. The views expressed in this work are solely those of the author and do not necessarily reflect the views of the publisher, and the publisher hereby disclaims any responsibility for them.

Any people depicted in stock imagery provided by Getty Images are models, and such images are being used for illustrative purposes only.
Certain stock imagery © Getty Images.

Scripture quotations are taken from the Holy Bible, New Living Translation, copyright © 1996, 2004, 2015 by Tyndale House Foundation. Used by permission of Tyndale House Publishers Inc., Carol Stream, Illinois 60188. All rights reserved.

ISBN: 979-8-3850-3298-3 (sc)
ISBN: 979-8-3850-3300-3 (hc)
ISBN: 979-8-3850-3299-0 (e)

Library of Congress Control Number: 2024918338

Print information available on the last page.

WestBow Press rev. date: 10/18/2024

WESTBOW
PRESS®
A DIVISION OF THOMAS NELSON
& ZONDERVAN

Olivia looked outside, watching water droplets race down the windowpane. It was the beginning of April...

Spring had sprung, and with it came pouring rains.

She waited for her mother, who was now
getting ready for Olivia's doctor visit.

While waiting, she wondered…she feared…she doubted.

Her worries just wouldn't quit:

What if something goes wrong?
What if it's worse than doctors think?
Every new wave of worry made her feel like she
would
sink.

Two months ago, the doctor had really bad news. The tummy aches Olivia suffered were not just stomach bug blues.

Doctor said it was serious. Something dangerous was inside. He said, "We may have to remove the growth."

She saw the concern her mother tried to hide.

Olivia hoped that just like the day's storm had passed, with the sun now peeking through the clouds...

Her sickness storm would end at last!

She could return to gymnastics and make her coaches proud.

"Olivia, make sure you have shoes on. I'm about ready to go!" her mom shouted from upstairs.

"I'm ready, Momma!" Olivia replied, hanging head low, trying not to show her cares.

"I'm ready for this storm of worry and sickness to end," she whispered as she rode to a doctor visit...

yet again.

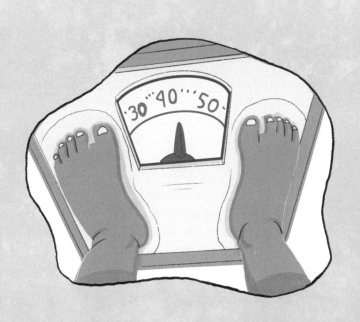

In and out of the hospital.
Many checkups, blood work, and scans too.

...waiting for the doctor to tell her mom
what else they could try to do.

It was a waiting game.
She was tired of waiting.
Olivia wanted the pain to end or at least to start fading.

Tick-Tock! Tick-Tock! The clock sounded extra loud in the waiting room than before.

Then suddenly out stepped a tall, joyful nurse from behind the waiting room door.

"Olivia!" she called, interrupting the ticking sound.
"Here!" her mother waved to the nurse.

Olivia's face frowned.

Vitals taken,
weight recorded,
blood work drawn again.

Olivia was ready for this sickness storm,
to finally come to an end.

Her mom combed her curls with her fingers as they waited for Dr. Terry to arrive. Olivia was tired of feeling so worried, so scared, so she sighed... and closed her eyes.

Immediately, she remembered her Grandma Rose, who had many doctor visits too. Oh, to hear what Grandma would say. Oh, to know what Grandma Rose would do.

Flashback: "Olivia," Grandma once said as they walked alone on the windy beach. "You see those waves out there, just beyond our reach?"

"Yes, Grandma. I see them. They are crashing on those rocks real strong."

"Yes, they are, my Sweet Liv,"
Grandma's voice trailed off.

"Grandma, what is wrong?"

"Olivia, I have something to share. You
know Grandma used to be quite ill?"

"Yes, Grandma; I was aware. We prayed for you to
heal." She continued, "Years ago we prayed for you,
and Grandma, you look great today to me."

"Sweetie, I was healed and even better in ways...doctors couldn't scan to see."

"You see, I prayed too, Sweet Liv...
but that is not all I would do":

"I praised God in the midst of that sickness
wave, and my peace was renewed."

"Thank you for believing with me that the attacking sickness wave would end. I knew that Jesus made a way for my healing. Oh, my faith would never bend."

"Still, Sweet Liv," Grandma continued, "Recall in the Bible when disciples met with the storm's attacking waves?"

"Jesus was asleep in the boat." Olivia smiled. "They woke Him up."

"Yes, Liv, to Jesus they called...

much like we pray today!"

"So, when attacking waves come our way, it's always good to *pray...*

and *praise*."

"Why?"

"Because mightier than the waves of the sea, is God's love for you and me."

"When we praise it quiets our worries and we experience God's peace."

"His love does heal.
His love does restore.
We pray for what we need, and we do something more":

"We praise Him.
We thank Him for what He's already done.
We praise Him in faith, knowing victory
over attacking waves...

"He's already won!"

"Liv, that day on the boat Jesus spoke to the waves,
'Peace be still.' In the same way, we can believe in
His love and might to give us peace and heal."

A year later her grandma, in her sleep, peacefully breathed her very last. And now as Olivia sat waiting, she knew what Grandma would say is her Sweet Liv's task:

Olivia rose, and asked her mom and doctor to be excused.

In the empty restroom she held her aching belly, with pain more than stomach bug blues. Looking at her reflection she whispered, "When attacking waves come our way, it's always good to *pray* and *praise*...

"Because mightier than the waves of the sea is God's love for you and me."

Then *prayed*, "Thank you, God, for all you have done. I believe by your stripes on the Cross I'm healed; I will overcome."

She *praised*, "My God, You're so big, so strong, and so mighty. There's nothing Your love cannot do."

She fought back the thoughts that tried to interrupt with: *"Olivia, that's just not true."*

Liv," Dr. Terry spoke as she returned to the room, "there's one more thing left to try."

A strong peace rushed over her. Before he went on, Olivia had faith she would live.

She would not die.

She smiled, and before leaving the room she
shook the doctor's hand with force.
Through *prayer* and *praise*, her faith in
God...was finally back on course.

She thought, *We believed with Grandma that God
still heals; today I will believe the same.*

*I will continue to pray...
AND praise, in Jesus' mighty name.*

Months later the doctor did another scan on her tummy. Olivia was nervous but strangely not worried in the least. It was through doing what Grandma Rose taught her—*pray* and *praise*—that she starved worry and received God's peace.

"When attacking waves come our way, it's always good to pray and praise..."

"Because mightier than the waves of the sea is God's love for you and me."

Days later, her mom answered a call
as Olivia drew nearby alone.

Suddenly, her mom cupped her lips, then
screamed, "LIV, THE GROWTH IS GONE!"

Olivia rushed to her side and hugged her mother tight. She knew from that day on what to do when attacking waves of sickness "pick a fight":

She would *pray*.
She would *praise*.
Her faith in God would then be raised.
And peace like a river would soon come.

When she was older,

she would also pray for others who experienced attacking
sickness waves, believing they too would overcome.

And when things didn't go the way she believed, by faith, in God's mighty love they would...

She would recall Grandma Rose's peace, as she looked at the crashing waves, and whisper...

"My God, you are still mighty."

"My God, you are still good."

AUTHOR'S NOTE

Dear Parents,

Welcome to *Olivia Braves Attacking Waves*, inspired by a summer camp curriculum I created in 2023. In this series, "attacking waves" symbolize life's challenges—bullying, family struggles, sickness, and negative thoughts—addressed through a biblically-based approach.

This book is the first in a 3-part series designed to help you engage your children in meaningful, intentional conversations:

- Series 1: Brave Attacking Waves (Matthew 8:23-27)
- Series 2: Brave Distracting Waves (Matthew 14:22-33)
- Series 3: Make Mighty Waves (John 4:1-29)

In *Olivia Braves Attacking Waves*, we explore sickness as an "attacking wave." My past experiences with illness have shown me that scripture is not just for memorization but for faith-filled activation in our day to day. Philippians 4:6-7 (NLT) has been particularly meaningful during difficult times:

"Don't worry about anything; instead, pray about everything. Tell God what you need, and thank him for all he has done. Then you will experience God's peace, which exceeds anything we can understand. His peace will guard your hearts and minds as you live in Christ Jesus."

As you read this book with your child, I hope you find opportunities to reflect on how you've faced life's challenges and be inspired to approach them with prayer and praise. Ultimately, my desire is that this book helps you guide the next generations to do the same, in Jesus' name.

Using This Book

- **Discussing Sickness and Faith:** Reflect on Olivia's experience to explore your own fears and uncertainties about illness. Share your experiences, encourage your child to share theirs, and guide them in turning to prayer and praise. (For more resources, visit www.rizngen.com)

- **The Power of Prayer and Praise:** Olivia's grandma teaches her to find peace through prayer and praise, even in sickness. Use this as a practical example of how faith can bring comfort and strength. (For more, visit www.rizngen.com)

- **Reflection and Application:** After reading, talk with your child about how they can apply these lessons in their lives. Explore situations where they might feel scared or worried and brainstorm ways to incorporate prayer and praise. (More resources at www.rizngen.com)

Key Verses

Olivia's lesson is grounded in three key Bible verses:

- **Psalm 93:4 (NIV)** - "Mightier than the thunder of the great waters, mightier than the breakers of the sea— the LORD on high is mighty."

- **Romans 8:37 (NLT)** - "No, despite all these things, overwhelming victory is ours through Christ, who loved us."

- **Philippians 4:6-7** - "Don't worry about anything; instead, pray about everything. Tell God what you need, and thank him for all he has done. Then you will experience God's peace, which exceeds anything we can understand. His peace will guard your hearts and minds as you live in Christ Jesus."

Let these verses guide your conversations and reinforce that God's love and power are greater than any challenges we face.

A Message of Hope

In short, this book is meant to offer hope and encouragement. Whether your child or someone they know is facing illness, Olivia's journey can inspire them to brave it with faith. Remember, *when attacking waves come our way, it's always good to pray and praise,* trusting that God's love is mightier than any storm we face.

Blessings on your Brave Journey,

Marissa Rose Aulick

INVITE THE AUTHOR FOR A FREE BOOK READING

Scan the QR code or email marissa.aulick@gmail.com to book a FREE reading of *Olivia Braves Attacking Waves: How She Faced Sickness with Faith* for your family, church, hospital, library, school, or community event. I'd love to bring the story to life and share its message of faith, hope, love, and resilience with your group!

Printed in the United States
by Baker & Taylor Publisher Services